For my sweet friend Allan,
my sister Louise,
and my teddy bear, Junior — CB

To my tangerine-bearded love — IM

Morris Micklewhite
and the Tangerine Dress

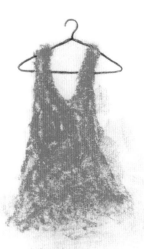

Christine Baldacchino

PICTURES BY
Isabelle Malenfant

GROUNDWOOD BOOKS
HOUSE OF ANANSI PRESS
TORONTO   BERKELEY

Morris Micklewhite has a mother named Moira
and a cat named Moo.

Morris likes Sundays
because his mother makes
him pancakes on Sundays.

Mondays are great, too, because on Mondays,
Morris goes to school.

Morris likes lots of things about school.

He likes to paint.

He likes to do puzzles.

He likes the apple juice
at snack time

and singing the loudest during circle time.

Most of all, Morris likes the dress-up center.
And the tangerine dress.
Morris likes the color of the dress.
It reminds him of tigers, the sun and his mother's hair.

He likes the noises the dress makes —
swish, swish, swish when he walks

and crinkle, crinkle, crinkle when he
sits down.

He takes turns wearing all the different shoes,
but his most favorite ones go click, click, click across
the floor.

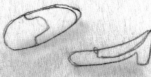

Sometimes the boys make fun of Morris.
Sometimes the girls do, too.

Morris pretends he can't hear their words
over the swish, swish, swishes,
crinkle, crinkle, crinkles,
and click, click, clicks he makes when he walks.
Morris pretends he can't hear their words, but he can.

On Monday, Becky tried to pull the dress right off his back.
"You can't wear it! You're a boy!"

On Tuesday, Eli, Henry and the other boys
wouldn't let Morris ride on their spaceship
unless he took the dress off.
"Astronauts don't wear dresses."

On Wednesday, Bea and Lila noticed Morris's fingernails.
His mother had painted them for him the night before.
They chased him around the playground shouting,
"Pinky Fingers! Pinky Fingers!"

On Thursday, the boys wouldn't sit near Morris at the snack table.
"We don't want you to turn us into girls."

On Friday, Morris pretended he had a tummy ache.
When he thought of all the kids in his class
and all the mean things they did and said,
his tummy ached for real.

His mother let him stay in his bed and read books about elephants.
Moo sat in his lap.
Moo liked elephants, too.

On Saturday, Morris's mother brought him
some apple juice.
As he took a sip, she stroked his hair.
Moo purred loudly.

Morris suddenly felt well enough to do a puzzle.
He hummed to himself, and felt better still.

On Sunday, Morris crawled out from under the covers
after a wonderful dream about being on a space safari with Moo.
In the dream, they saw big blue elephants,
and tigers the color of the sun that Morris could hold
in the palm of his hand.

The elephants swish, swish, swished as they moved through the grass,
and the tigers ate giant leaves that crinkle, crinkle, crinkled
as their tiny teeth chewed them.
The buttons on the spaceship click, click, clicked under Morris's fingers.

Morris wanted to share
all the amazing things he had seen.
He took out his brushes, put on his smock and began to paint,
using every color he could imagine.

He showed his painting to his mother when he was done.
He pointed out the big blue elephant,
the tiny tiger the color of the sun,
the tall grass and the giant leaves.
He pointed out Moo in his shiny round space helmet.

"And who's that?" his mother asked,
pointing at the little boy in the tangerine dress
riding atop the big blue elephant.
Morris was hoping she'd ask.
"That's me," he said.

On Monday, Morris went to school
with his painting rolled up in his backpack.
When he had the chance,
he put on the dress that reminded him of tigers
and the sun
and his mother's hair.

Morris swish, swish, swished.
The tangerine dress crinkle, crinkle, crinkled.
His shoes click, click, clicked.
Morris felt wonderful.

Eli and Henry wouldn't let him on their spaceship,
so Morris built his own.
He hung his painting on the front of it and climbed in,
ready to take off.

"Are there really elephants in space?" Eli asked.

"And tigers?"

"If you follow me, we can find out,"
Morris offered.

Eli and Henry followed Morris to a planet they had
never visited before.
As they explored, Morris swish, swish, swished.
The tangerine dress crinkle, crinkle, crinkled.
His shoes click, click, clicked.

By the time they returned to Earth, Eli and Henry had decided
that it didn't matter if astronauts wore dresses or not.
The best astronauts were the ones who knew
where all the good adventures were hiding.
Morris smiled. He already knew that.

When snack time was over, Becky demanded the dress.
Morris told her she could have it when he was done with it.
"Boys don't wear dresses," Becky snipped.
Morris smiled as he swished, crinkled and clicked back to
his spaceship.
"This boy does."

Groundwood Books / House of Anansi Press
110 Spadina Avenue, Suite 801, Toronto, Ontario M5V 2K4
or c/o Publishers Group West
1700 Fourth Street, Berkeley, CA 94710

We acknowledge for their financial support of our publishing program
the Canada Council for the Arts, the Government of Canada through
the Canada Book Fund (CBF) and the Ontario Arts Council.

 Canada Council Conseil des Arts
for the Arts du Canada

 ONTARIO ARTS COUNCIL
CONSEIL DES ARTS DE L'ONTARIO

Library and Archives Canada Cataloguing in Publication
Baldacchino, Christine, author
Morris Micklewhite and the tangerine dress / by Christine
Baldacchino ; illustrated by Isabelle Malenfant.
Issued in print and electronic formats.
ISBN 978-1-55498-347-6 (bound). — ISBN 978-1-55498-350-6 (html)
I. Malenfant, Isabelle, illustrator II. Title.
PS8603.A527M67 2014   jC813'.6   C2013-905603-3
C2013-905604-1

The illustrations were done in charcoal, watercolor, pastel
and Adobe Photoshop.
Design by Michael Solomon
Printed and bound in Malaysia

4|15